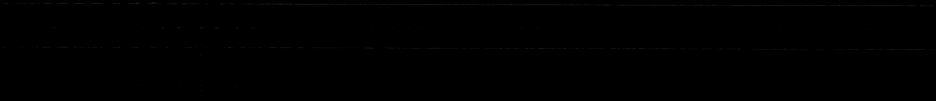

This is the
true story
of Heidi.
She will steal
your heart,
as well as
your blanket.

Heidi has always loved blankets. When she was little, she loved to curl up inside them.

The very first blanket she stole was underneath her sister. She tugged and tugged with her little teeth until she got that blanket.

Then she started stealing blankets from her other sisters and brothers.

She stole blankets from her mommy and daddy, especially on cold nights.

She stole blankets from visiting cousins.

She stole blankets from visiting friends.

She even stole a blanket from a baby!

Sometimes, she would roll until she was wrapped up in the blanket like **a mummy**. It was very hard to get the blanket back when she was so wrapped up in it. It felt like she was stuck to the blanket with **glue!**

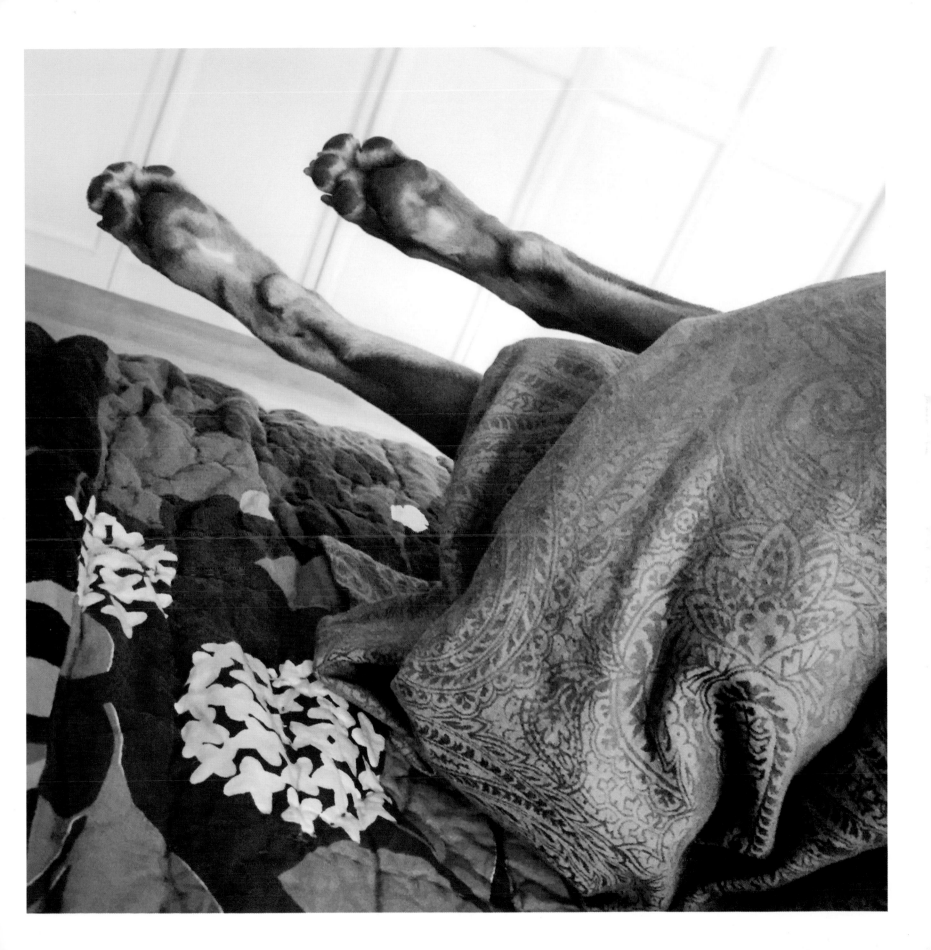

Her mommy and daddy would try to unroll her – Mommy taking both front paws and Daddy taking both back paws, gently rolling her in one direction and rolling and rolling until the blanket was free.

Sometimes, they gave up because they were so tired and they would curl up on either side of her.

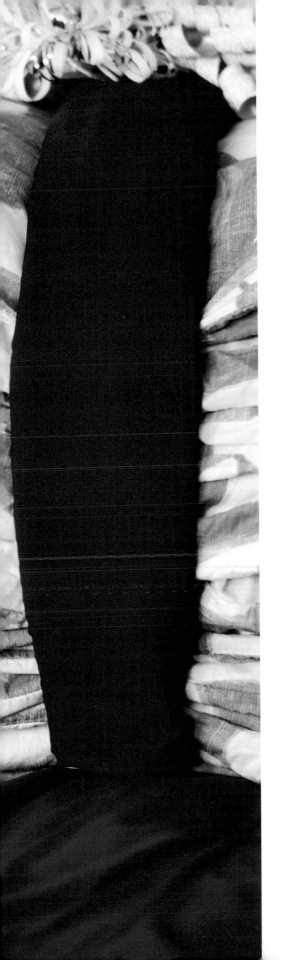

Then, one day, her mommy came home with **the biggest blanket** Heidi had ever seen! It was a huge, fluffy comforter for their bed.

The new blanket was too long to roll in and it was too big to steal.

There was only one solution. Heidi had to go underneath the new blanket. She used her nose as a drill to lift the comforter and then she wiggled and wiggled until she disappeared.

It was so much fun!
Even more fun than
stealing it!

Now, when she watches television, or has a slumber party, or is in bed for the night, Heidi gets right in the middle and nuzzles her way under the blanket, no matter how small or large.

Finally, everyone is warm and happy.

Well, almost everyone.

Special Thanks

to family and friends who made this book possible.

Thank you to my incredibly supportive husband, Joseph.
Thank you to my son, Joseph, for endless inspiration,
encouragement, and sharing your many talents.

Copyright © 2019 by Lori Anne Dryer
All rights reserved. No part of this publication
may be reproduced, distributed or transmitted
in any form or by any means without the prior
written permission of the publisher.

PHOTOGRAPHY

front cover, pages 5, 13, 18, 26, 29, 30, 33, 40 by **Mannat Kaur**
(see more of her work on Instagram at **@Mannatphoto**);
back cover, pages 1, 6, 9, 10, 14, 17, 21, 22, 25, 34, 37, 38
by **Lori Anne Dryer**

Library of Congress Cataloging-in-Publication
Data available.

ISBN: 978-1-949480-04-7

10 9 8 7 6 5 4 3 2 1

Manufactured in China

Design by **Masayo Ozawa, A Bomb In A Bull**
www.abombinabull.com

See Heidi in action at **www.TheBlanketThief.net**

 Roundtree Press

149 Kentucky Street, Suite 7, Petaluma, CA 94952